Night Frights

THIRTEEN SCARY STORIES

J.B. STAMPER

AN
APPLE
PAPERBACK

SCHOLASTIC INC.
New York Toronto London Auckland Sydney

ISBN 0-590-46046-3

12 11 10 9   5 6 7 8/9

Printed in the U.S.A.   40

First Scholastic printing, February 1993

Contents

Graveyard Dare   1

Bloody Mary   8

Cold, Bony Fingers   15

The Mysterious Visitor   22

The Witch's Paw   27

The Corpse's Revenge   32

Coming to Get You   36

Stop That Coffin   44

Nightmare   48

The Stranger   54

Mummies   59

Bloody Bones   65

Night Woods   71

Graveyard Dare

The four boys had dragged their sleeping bags and pillows up to the top floor of the old house. They had brought along flashlights because there wasn't any electricity in the attic. Now they were sitting around talking by the eerie glow of the lights. One of the boys — his name was Andrew — went over to the small window in one of the house's gables and peered out.

"Look, you can see that old graveyard from here," he said.

His friends, Tommy, Mark, and Richard, crowded behind him to stare out the small panes of the window.

"You can even see the tombstones," Mark said. "They're all white in the moonlight, like ghosts."

"My dad told me some old stories about that graveyard," Richard said, "when we first moved into this house. He said I should keep out of it at night."

Andrew turned to Richard with a look of disgust. "And you're probably too scared to go in there, anyway. It's only a graveyard with a bunch of dead people's skeletons a couple of feet under the ground. Do you think they're going to rise up and get you?"

The other three boys laughed nervously. Then Mark said in a low voice, "Why don't you go out there right now if you think you're so brave?"

Everyone turned to watch Andrew's face. He had picked up his flashlight again, and the eerie light was shining on his features. All of a sudden, a strange grin came over his face and he said, "Okay, I'll show you guys. I'll do it. You can watch me from up here."

"Come on, Mark was just kidding," Richard said. "And anyway, if my parents found out about this, I'd be grounded forever."

"How would they find out?" Andrew said, pulling on his sneakers.

"Listen, how will we know that you really go in?" Mark said. "You could just go down there, but never go inside the cemetery. I want proof."

"Like what?" Andrew said. "A skeleton?"

"I've got an idea," Richard said. "There's that old white birch tree that grows right in the middle of the cemetery. You've all seen it, right? It's the only birch tree growing in the whole town. So if Andrew breaks off a branch and brings it back here, we'll know from the white bark that he was inside the cemetery."

2

"It's a deal," Mark said.

"A deal," Andrew echoed.

Richard went down the stairs with Andrew to help him slip out the back door of the house.

"Hey, you don't really have do to this," Richard said. "We can all just forget about it, you know."

"Just go back upstairs and wait for me," Andrew said. "I'm not afraid of a graveyard at night." Then he slipped away into the shadows of the big trees that grew around Richard's house.

It was colder out than Andrew had expected. He felt the wind cut through his thin jacket as he circled around Richard's house and took the sidewalk that led to the old church. He was only a few yards away from it when the bell high in the old tower began to ring. The sound of the bell echoed through the night, over and over, one . . . two . . . three. . . . It kept up until it had struck twelve. Andrew's ears were still ringing after the bell had stopped, and his whole body seemed to be shaking. The bell's vibration had set his nerves on edge, especially when he realized it was after midnight.

Andrew crept around the side of the stone walls of the church, heading for the low iron fence that surrounded the cemetery. Just as he drew near the gate, he heard a strange rustling sound, like animals moving in the night or branches clawing against a wall. For a second he stopped, his heart in his throat. Then he looked up and saw Richard's house in the distance. The glow of three flashlights shone in the high attic window. Andrew knew he had to go on, or he would never live it down.

The gate in the iron fence was locked, just as Andrew thought it would be. He had seen a church custodian lock it up at nightfall before. He felt the sharp tips at the top of the fence's iron bars and paused to think. Then he backed up, took a running jump, and vaulted over the fence. His feet hit the soft grass of the graveyard on the other side and seemed to sink in.

Andrew stood perfectly still for a minute, listening and looking around him. Suddenly, everything seemed different. Outside, the graveyard had looked harmless and, well, dead. But inside — inside the locked fence — it was different. The tombstones stood higher in the moonlight than he expected. Some of them were even taller than he was. They seemed to loom toward him, their cold, white marble glowing in the night.

Andrew began to walk among them toward the center of the graveyard. He couldn't seem to find a path and had to walk over the soft, soggy ground. As he picked his way through the tombstones, a small, low stone caught at his foot like a trap. Andrew stopped and suddenly heard a rattling sound behind him. He whirled around, but saw nothing except a large tomb with a carved face staring back at him. The hair on the back of his neck seemed to stand up on end, and his body began to shiver even harder from the cold wind.

Andrew started to run through the tombstones, anxious to reach the birch tree and carry out his dare. He told himself that he was letting his imagination go wild. But with every step he took, he seemed to hear a strange noise behind him. Yet when he turned around to look, all he saw were the tombstones sitting like cold, silent guards over the dead.

Finally, several yards ahead, he saw the old birch tree, its white branches shining in the moonlight. Andrew knew he only had to go a little further, and he would get what he had come for.

A low, whooing sound vibrated through the air, sending chills through Andrew's body. It was an owl, he told himself, just an owl. He looked up at a tree above him and caught sight of the moon. A dark cloud was beginning to move across it. Andrew started to run faster toward the birch tree. He was almost to it when, suddenly, he tripped on a low tombstone and sprawled face down on the soft, damp ground of the cemetery. And when he looked up and pulled himself to his feet, the moon had gone under the cover of the cloud.

Andrew put both hands out in front of him and stumbled forward. It was pitch-black in the graveyard now. Then, suddenly, his right hand touched something cold and hard. He reached out for it with both hands and felt it. It must be a branch

5

of the birch tree, he told himself. He grabbed hold of a thick part of it, and with a quick jerk, pulled. With a loud crack, it broke off in his hands. Suddenly sick with fear, Andrew pushed it under one arm and started to run.

He wasn't sure which way to go. All he cared about was getting out of the cemetery. The strange whooing sound was getting louder and louder now, and rustling and rattling sounds were all around him. He couldn't see where he was going as he ran. Twice he stumbled and fell face down on the soggy earth. But he never let go of the birch branch tucked under his arm. He was determined to show his friends that he'd completed the dare.

Andrew looked up and saw the shadowy hulk of the church looming in front of him. Then he felt his body bump right into the fence that surrounded the graveyard. He had to step back to get a running start to clear the fence. But as he backed up, he felt something grab at his coat. It tugged and tugged and seemed to try to pull him back into the graveyard. Andrew screamed and shook whatever it was off him. Then he started to run and, just as something grabbed at the back of his neck, he jumped and cleared the fence.

He never stopped running until he reached Richard's back door. He pushed open the door and stumbled into the house, still clutching the birch branch. He ran up the three flights of stairs to the attic where his friends were waiting.

They stood there, their flashlights casting pools of light in the dark room.

"I got it," he panted, "I got it." Then he pulled the branch from under his arm and held it above his head.

The room was filled by a horrible silence. Mark, Tommy, and Richard didn't say a word. They stood staring at the thing he was holding with looks of terror on their faces. Andrew followed their eyes up to the cold, hard object he held in his trembling hands.

And he saw that it was the arm of a skeleton . . . its bony fingers dangling down into his face.

Bloody Mary

The five girls were sleeping over in an old house that belonged to one of their grandmothers. The house was big and drafty, but the friends were gathered around a fireplace in the study. Michelle threw another log on the fire to keep it going, and they all watched as the embers glowed brighter and the orange-tipped flames jumped up from the dry wood. Suddenly, there was a loud crack as the wood began to burn, making everyone jump and laugh nervously.

"Want to tell scary stories?" Michelle asked in a soft whisper.

At first everyone was quiet and just looked at each other's faces in the firelight.

"My older sister told me one last weekend," Kate said. "It's called Bloody Mary."

Everyone stared at Mary. Then Michelle grabbed her hand and said, "Look, no blood."

"I'm not talking about our Mary," Kate said. "I

8

mean the real Bloody Mary — she was Queen of England a long time ago."

"So why was she called Bloody Mary?" Ellen asked.

"Because she liked to chop off people's heads, that's why. If someone didn't do what Bloody Mary wanted, she had them condemned to death. They were led to a chopping block. They had to put their heads on the block, and then an executioner with a black hood over his head came up with a big, shiny ax. And, chop! Their heads would roll off."

Screams of disgust filled the room.

"But that's not all," Kate went on. "There's an old superstition about Bloody Mary."

All the girls drew closer to hear what Kate was going to say. Especially Mary. She loved to hear scary stories. And she'd never heard about Bloody Mary before.

"They say," Kate began again, "that Bloody Mary still comes back. They say that if you go into a room with a mirror at night, and you turn off all the lights, Bloody Mary will appear."

Kate stopped for a few seconds and looked around at her friends' faces. All their eyes were staring at her, and Mary's, in particular, looked strangely shiny and excited.

"So you stand in the dark, dark room with no lights on — right in front of the mirror. And you begin to chant the words, 'I do believe in Bloody Mary, I do believe in Bloody Mary . . . ' over and over again. Then, if you've done everything just right, Bloody Mary's face will slowly appear in the mirror. And finally, you'll find out why she's really called Bloody Mary."

Kate stopped talking, and all the girls but Mary started to make scary sounds and talk about what Bloody Mary might look like. But Mary sat quietly in the dark, staring into the jumping flames of the fireplace. For a second, she thought she saw a face there, staring back at her. But, suddenly, the fire made a loud crack and the log broke in two, sending a shower of embers up into the fireplace. Mary gasped and shook her head, as though she were coming out of a dream.

"Look at Mary!" Michelle said. "She looks bloody!"

Everyone started to scream and laugh. Mary had drawn so close to the fire that her face was flushed red, and the shadows of the flickering flames made her face look as though it were streaked with blood. Mary felt her hot cheeks and drew back from the fire into a dark corner where her sleeping bag was spread out. The other girls started to tell another scary story, but Mary couldn't concentrate on what they were saying. Her eyes grew heavy, and in her mind, a shadowy face appeared and disappeared until it became part of her dreams.

*   *   *

Mary woke up with a start, confused about where she was. She sat up and stared into the darkness until her eyes picked out the tiny, bright glow of a few dying embers in the fireplace. At first, Mary thought they were animal eyes staring at her; then, suddenly, she remembered where she was. At a sleepover . . . at Michelle's grandmother's house. As her eyes slowly became more accustomed to the darkness, Mary could make out the sleeping figures of her four friends, huddled around the fireplace in their sleeping bags. Then, with a shock, she remembered Bloody Mary. The story seemed so real now, as though she had heard it only minutes ago. Then she remembered her dreams, how Bloody Mary had haunted her sleep.

Suddenly an idea crept into Mary's mind. It wrapped itself around her brain and wouldn't let go. She tried to force the thought away by concentrating on something else. But it always came back, stronger than before. The thought told her to find out if the story was true. To call to Bloody Mary in a dark room in front of a mirror. To see what happened.

Almost against her will, Mary pulled her legs out of the warm sleeping bag and stood up in the shadowy room. She began to walk across the room, stepping over the bodies of her sleeping friends. Mary reached the door to the study,

11

pulled it open, and walked through. She found herself standing at the bottom of the creaky staircase that climbed up to the second floor.

Quietly, like a cat, she crept up the stairs to the landing. The first door on the right was closed; Mary knew it was the room where Michelle's grandmother slept. She turned to the left down the hall and kept walking until she came to the very last door. Slowly and carefully, she turned the knob and stepped inside. Mary shut the door behind her and felt for a light switch on the wall. For a brief moment, light flooded the room, long enough for Mary to see the big mirror in an old-fashioned frame hanging on the wall across the room. She flicked the lights back off and, like a sleepwalker, moved slowly but deliberately toward the mirror. She reached out in the darkness and touched its cold, smooth surface a foot away from where she stopped.

Just then, the moon broke through the clouds in the night sky and a thin shaft of moonlight pierced the darkness of the room. Mary gasped as she saw a face appear in the mirror. Then, as she watched the face slowly smile, she realized that it was her own.

The story isn't true, she told herself. It's just a silly superstition. Then she remembered the words. She hadn't said the words yet. She hadn't called for Bloody Mary.

She raised her hands toward the mirror and slowly began to chant, "I do believe in Bloody Mary . . . I do believe in Bloody Mary."

She kept staring into the mirror, but only her face — with frightened-looking eyes — stared back at her.

"I do believe in Bloody Mary . . . I do believe in Bloody Mary."

The eyes in the mirror didn't look frightened anymore. They were hard and seemed to glow. Mary didn't understand why her mouth was turning down in such a wicked smile, but she kept chanting.

"I do believe in Bloody Mary . . . I do believe in Bloody Mary."

Mary saw that the face in the mirror had skin that was pocked and spotted with a rough, red rash. And the hair seemed to curl out of the head like black snakes!

"I do believe in Bloody Mary . . . I do believe in Bloody Mary," her voice kept chanting.

And then, suddenly, two hands — two bloody hands — reached up beside the face in the mirror. Mary stopped chanting and a scream started to rise in her throat. She stared at the face of Bloody Mary in the mirror and saw the bloody hands reach right out of the mirror toward her.

The bloody hands grabbed hold of Mary's neck as she began to scream and scream and scream.

When her friends flicked on the light in the bedroom, they saw Mary suddenly collapse onto the floor in front of the mirror. Running over to her, they saw the blood smeared around her neck. Then Mary looked up at them with crazed eyes and began to chant over and over again, "I do believe in Bloody Mary . . . I do believe in Bloody Mary . . . I do believe in Bloody Mary."

The friends looked into the mirror on the wall. But the face of Bloody Mary was gone. All they saw were their own faces — with frightened eyes — staring back at them.

Cold, Bony Fingers

Tomás liked to walk with his grandfather in the high, windswept hills that surrounded the small town where he lived. The hills were cut into strange shapes by the wind that had been blowing over them for more centuries than Tomás could imagine. His grandfather told Tomás about the ancient peoples who lived in the hills and were probably still buried there.

Tomás listened to his grandfather's stories, but he didn't believe all of them, especially the ones about the dead people. Tomás wasn't the least bit superstitious, and his grandfather's stories were full of warnings about ghosts and evil spirits.

One day, Tomás went out walking in the hills by himself. His grandfather wasn't feeling well because his legs were stiff and ached. Tomás promised to bring back a special plant that helped cure the aching. It grew wild in the hills where he and his grandfather often took their walks.

Tomás set off from the town on a trail that

wound up through the reddish-brown soil into the mountains. He decided to go visit the sheltered, cavelike hollows that the wind had carved into one of the hills many centuries ago. As he walked, he was surprised to find so many rocks fallen on the trail. He remembered hearing the wind last night when it woke him from a deep sleep. But the storm must have been much worse than he realized to have loosened so much dirt and rock from the mountain.

Tomás walked on, glancing around for the plant that he had promised to bring his grandfather. But he remembered that it grew much higher on the mountain, close to where the hollows were. As he climbed up the trail, Tomás hugged his jacket tighter around his body. The wind was still blowing hard, and it cut through his clothes like a knife. Tomás started to run to stay warm. Soon, he came to an overlook and stopped to rest.

Below him in the valley, Tomás saw his town. It looked so small and unimportant from where he stood. And, suddenly, Tomás felt small and unimportant, too, all alone on the mountain. He shivered and thought about turning around and running back home. But he remembered the plant he'd promised to get his grandfather and started back up the mountain trail.

A short time later, Tomás came to the place where another small trail led off toward the hollowed-out caves in the side of the mountain. He could see that the windstorm had been even stronger here. Loose soil and rock were blown into piles where they'd never been before.

Finally, Tomás reached the base of one of the hollows. It looked like a dark mouth carved into the side of the mountain. He began to climb up a steep rise to its entrance, but halfway up he came to a sudden stop.

Right in front of him on the trail was a white object. It was so white that it seemed to be shining in the sun. Tomás stared at it in disbelief. He'd climbed this rise many times with his grandfather. But he'd never seen this skull before.

Tomás stepped up to the skull and then bent down on his knees to study it. The skull lay looking back up at him with its empty eyes and grinning teeth. Tomás reached down to pick it up and, just as he touched the hard, smooth bone, he remembered his grandfather's words. Never take bones from a dead body. Do not disturb the rest of the dead.

For a moment, Tomás almost dropped the skull. He could still hear the warning note in his grandfather's voice. But now the skull was in his hands, and he wanted to keep it. He could hide it on the bottom shelf of his bedroom closet. And when his friends came over, he could show it to them. No one he knew had a human skull.

The skull grinned up at him as Tomás carried it away from the mountain. He knew that the rest

17

of its skeleton was buried somewhere nearby, and the grave had been disturbed by the storm the night before. But now the skull was his. And, after all, whomever it belonged to was long, long dead.

When Tomás came near his house, he pushed the skull under his jacket and then hurried into his room and hid it. Then he came out to talk to his grandfather, who sat rocking in a chair by the big living-room window. The moment he met his grandfather's eyes, he remembered the plant he'd promised to bring.

"I'm sorry, Grandpa. . . . I forgot the plant. But I can go back to get it, if you want," Tomás stuttered, suddenly feeling as though everything he'd done was wrong.

His grandfather told him it was too late today, but maybe tomorrow he could go back for the plant. Tomás agreed and then went back to his room. He looked again at the skull, grinning out at him from its hiding place. Suddenly, Tomás wished he hadn't brought it home. He threw a sweater over it and shut the closet door.

That night, the wind began to howl again. Tomás went to bed early because his parents had gone out and his grandfather had started telling stories again. Tomás didn't want to hear the stories. He'd lied and said he didn't feel well. But when he laid down in bed, it didn't seem to be a lie anymore. He didn't feel well. His body felt shivery and his stomach ached, and the thought of the skull in the closet filled his mind with an uneasy dread.

Finally, he couldn't stand to just lie in the dark anymore and think about the skull. He got up, turned on the lights, and opened his closet door. He picked up the sweater he'd thrown over it and saw the skull sitting there, just where he'd left it. It was still grinning at him, but now the grin seemed to have an evil edge to it. Tomás slammed the closet door and ran back to his bed, flicking off the light and covering his head with his blanket. After tossing and turning for more than an hour, he fell asleep at last.

Tomás wasn't sure what woke him hours later in the middle of the night. Maybe it was the wind still howling outside. Or maybe it was the aching feeling in his stomach. But whatever it was made him sit bolt upright in bed.

He sat there in bed, feeling a shiver travel through his whole body from head to toe. Then he noticed the strange smell in the room, the smell of something old . . . and dead. And as he sat there in the dark, shaking, Tomás heard a strange sound. It was the sound of things that were smooth and hard, clicking against each other. With trembling hands, Tomás reached over and turned on his light. And standing at the end of his bed, Tomás saw a headless skeleton. Its long, bony arms were reaching out and seemed to be searching for something.

Then, from inside his closet, Tomás heard a weird voice call, "Give me back my bones. Give me back my bones."

Tomás shrank down in the bed. He watched as the white skeleton moved around his room, grasping out with its bony fingers. The legs stalked over to where he lay, and the cold, bony fingers touched his feet. And, still, from the closet, came the voice, "Give me back my bones. Give me back my bones."

Then the bony fingers of the skeleton moved up to Tomás's head and felt his eyes and nose and lips. Fear choked Tomás's voice and he lay there, unable to scream, waiting for the skeleton to take its revenge.

But the voice from the closet called out louder, "Give me back my bones. Give me back my bones."

Suddenly Tomás jumped from his bed and ran to the closet. He opened the door and reached down to pick up the cold, white skull. Its hollow sockets looked up at him, and its grinning teeth began to move.

"Give me back my bones. Give me back my bones."

Tomás's hands were shaking, but he carried the skull to the skeleton and placed it on top of the neck. The skull turned its face to him and grinned once more. Then the skeleton walked out of Tomás's room.

*   *   *

The next morning, Tomás woke with an awful headache. He rubbed his eyes in the morning sun, and suddenly remembered the terrible dream he'd had. Then the memory came back so strong that Tomás began to tremble. It *was* a dream, wasn't it?

He jumped out of bed and ran to his closet. He searched and searched. But the grinning skull was . . . gone.

The Mysterious Visitor

Amy's eyes wandered from her book to look out the high windows of the living room. Nothing was there, just snowflakes lightly falling through the sky. Still Amy shivered. She felt uneasy and a little scared, all alone in the Morgan's big house. Little Isabelle, the baby, was sound asleep in her nursery upstairs. Amy almost wished the baby would wake up. At least there would be human sounds in the house to keep her company.

Amy tried to keep her attention on the history book she was reading. Her teacher had warned the class that there might be a quiz on Monday morning. But it was difficult to concentrate, and Amy's eyes kept wandering off the page to look out into the dark night.

She must have gone into a daze, staring out the window at the lightly falling snowflakes. Because, suddenly, every muscle in her body jumped when she heard the sound of the front door opening.

Amy listened to the click of the latch and then the slight creak of the heavy door as it moved. She even felt a cold draft move through the living room just as she heard the door shut again.

"Mrs. Morgan?" she called out in a frightened voice. "Mr. Morgan?"

There was no answer. Only a dead silence in the big house.

Amy felt her heart begin to pound. Could it have been the wind that pushed the door open and closed? Or had someone come into the house?

Amy shrank into a ball on the couch. She was suddenly afraid to move. Then she heard something that made her blood run cold. Footsteps. Heavy footsteps were moving across the hallway toward the staircase.

"Who is it?" Amy called out, her voice trembling.

There was no answer, only the sound of the footsteps slowly climbing the stairs to the second floor. Amy was so afraid now that she felt sick. She sat on the couch, listening to the footsteps clump up one step after another, higher and higher on the staircase.

Then, suddenly, through the panic clogging her mind, she remembered the baby. Isabelle. Amy knew she couldn't just hide from the footsteps. She had to make sure the baby was all right.

Standing up on trembling legs, Amy began to creep quietly across the living room toward the

23

hallway. Just as she peeked around the corner of the doorway, she heard the footsteps reach the top of the stairs and begin to move across the upstairs floor. Then they stopped.

Amy froze where she stood. Terrible thoughts flew through her mind. She knew she couldn't wait any longer. She had to go up and check on Isabelle. Amy pushed the thought of the footsteps out of her mind and raced up the staircase as fast as she could climb the steps. Her heart was pounding, and her breath was coming in short gasps by the time she got to the top. Several lights were turned on in the hallway, and Amy searched every doorway and corner. But she saw no one there.

Quickly, she dashed to the doorway of Isabelle's room. She flicked on the light and looked around. The room was empty except for the baby, and she was cuddled in one corner of her crib, sound asleep. Amy strained her ears. There was no sound except for Isabelle's light breathing. No footsteps. No hints of danger.

For a second, Amy wondered if it had all been her imagination. Had she really heard the door open? Had she really heard the footsteps on the stairs? Maybe she had fallen asleep and it had been part of a bad dream.

Amy looked at the baby one more time and then turned off the light. She tried to walk slowly down the hallway to the stairs, but halfway there she began to run, and she scrambled down the stairs so fast that she almost fell. Finally, she ran into the living room and jumped back onto the sofa, curling her feet under her. She felt as though she'd just had a terrible nightmare, but now it was over.

With trembling hands, Amy picked up her book again. But a second later, she heard the sound. The sound of the footsteps. They were coming back down the stairs. Clump. Clump. Clump.

Amy wanted to scream out, but her throat had gone dry and tight. She listened to the footsteps get louder and louder as they came closer and closer to the hallway. In horror, she turned to look through the doorway to the staircase. The footsteps sounded as if they had just reached the bottom of the steps and were coming across the hallway toward her. But she could see nothing, nothing at all.

Amy fixed her eyes on that terrifying, empty space where the footsteps had stopped, just at the doorway to the living room where she sat. For several agonizing moments, there was silence.

Then the footsteps turned away and walked toward the front door. The door latch clicked and, once again, the solid wooden door swung open. Amy heard the heavy footsteps walk outside. Then the door shut . . . and the house was filled with silence.

Slowly, Amy stood up and began to walk toward the front door. She walked over to the place at the doorway where the footsteps had waited.

Then she went to the front door and slowly, carefully opened it. The snow was swirling down in big, thick flakes now.

Amy looked down at the sidewalk. In the snow she saw large, deep footprints — walking away from the house.

The Witch's Paw

The winter days were long and lonely in the Tennessee hills, but the nights were even longer. Matt lived on a remote farm in a deep valley surrounded by mountains that hunched up against the sky. One night, he sat around the fireplace with his father and Jeb Adams, a neighbor who had come to visit. His mother and Mrs. Adams were busy in the kitchen.

"It's that time again," Jeb said, "when the witch-cat starts to prowl."

Matt turned his eyes from the fire to stare at Jeb's face and then his father's. He saw that his father had raised his eyebrows at Jeb, as a signal to be quiet.

"The boy should know," Jeb said. "Especially with you and his mother going off to the state capital next week. He should know about the witch-cat."

Just then Matt's mother came into the room

with Mrs. Adams, whose sharp green eyes measured Matt up and down.

"Time to go home," she announced. "We'll be back soon enough to pick up Matt when you take your trip to the capital."

As soon as the Adamses left, Matt followed his father outside to the stable. He had to feed the new colt his father had given him. And he also wanted to hear about the witch-cat.

"Your mother doesn't want you to know about this, boy," his father said. "But maybe Jeb's right. This witch has been prowling around these hills for over twenty years. I say prowling because she changes shape from a woman into a big, black cat. This is not a natural-size cat, mind you, but a big, black cat the size of a hunting dog. People who've seen the witch say her eyes glow yellow in the night and her teeth are like fangs. The witch-cat kills livestock, even horses."

Matt's father stopped when he saw Matt staring down at the small colt.

"We'll only be gone two days," he said. "Don't you worry yourself."

On the day his parents left, Mrs. Adams came to the house without Jeb. She told Matt that her husband was too busy with his livestock to come over and get him. They'd decided she would stay the night with Matt at his house.

Matt didn't like the idea. But since his parents were already on their way, he couldn't do anything about it. He spent the day doing his chores and, that night, he sat around the fire with Mrs. Adams. For a March night, it had gotten very cold with a gusty wind whipping around the sides of the house.

"Hear about the witch-cat?" Mrs. Adams suddenly said. "It's prowling around again."

"Where?" Matt asked, hoping his voice wasn't shaking.

"On the other side of Pepper Hill, last night," Mrs. Adams said. "It killed a calf."

Matt shivered and pulled his wool sweater tighter around his neck. He thought of the little colt alone in the stable outside.

Mrs. Adams suddenly yawned and stretched her arms and legs. She told Matt that she was ready to turn in for the night. But he noticed that her eyes were bright and shiny, like she wasn't tired at all. Still, he got ready to go to bed. She watched as he climbed the flight of wooden steps up into the loft bedroom. Then he heard her close the door to his parents' bedroom where she was sleeping.

Matt couldn't go to sleep, no matter how many sheep he counted. The wind was whining and moaning now, and the glass rattled in the windowpanes. Then a sound came out of the night that made his blood run cold.

It was the meow of a cat. But it was so loud that Matt heard it over the moaning of the wind.

The meowing kept on and on, moving around the outside of the house. Matt raised himself up on his trembling elbows and turned his head toward the small window that looked out over the barnyard.

It was there in the moonlight, the shadowy shape of a huge, black cat. Matt watched as it slowly raised its head toward the second story of the house where he lay. He saw its yellow eyes glowing in the moonlight. Then, as Matt watched, the witch-cat turned away and began to stalk toward the stable.

The colt. Suddenly, Matt knew what the witch-cat was after. It wanted his colt. He jumped up and pulled on his clothes and boots. He scrambled down the steps and called out Mrs. Adams's name. But there was no answer.

Just then, Matt heard a terrible screech from the witch-cat, closer now to the colt's stable. He pulled on a jacket and reached for the big hunting knife that his father kept by the door. Grabbing it tightly, he pulled open the door.

The March wind cut into his face as Matt rushed across the barnyard toward the stable. As he drew closer, he saw that the stable door was standing open. He swallowed the lump of fear that had risen in his throat and crept inside.

The moonlight was shining down through a window into the colt's pen. Matt saw the colt, cowering in a corner. In front of it was the big witch-cat. Its long, sharp fangs glistened as it snarled at the colt.

Just as the witch-cat leapt forward, Matt lunged at it with his hunting knife. The knife sliced down on its right front paw. Blood spurted out. Matt jumped back as the witch-cat screamed in pain. Then he looked down and saw the pool of blood on the stable floor.

Matt watched as the witch-cat limped out of the stable, hissing and snarling. When it was gone, he stooped down to pet his colt. Seeing the blood nearby, he kicked straw over it in disgust.

Suddenly, Matt began to shake with cold and fear. He wanted to be back inside the house, safe and warm. He pulled shut the stable door and bolted it. Then he ran through the shadows of the barnyard into the house. He remembered as he closed the kitchen door that he had left the hunting knife in the stable.

A strange sound came from near the fireplace. Matt raised his eyes to see Mrs. Adams sitting in front of the leaping flames. The sound he heard was a weird hissing coming from her mouth. Her eyes seemed to be glowing yellow in the fire-light.

And then Matt noticed her right hand. It was slowly dripping blood onto the farmhouse floor.

The Corpse's Revenge

Henry Archer woke with a start, feeling as though he were coming out of a long nightmare. He remembered that he had been sick for weeks, deathly sick. He remembered the doctor standing over his bed and shaking his head, as though there were no hope. The faces of his nephews were there, too, their glittering eyes staring down at his weak body. At the time, Henry's confused thoughts had cleared enough to realize that they wanted him to die, wanted him dead so they could inherit all his money.

Now Henry felt better than he had during all those long weeks of illness. The only problem he seemed to be having was a certain shortness of breath. And the night was so dark, and his bed felt unusually hard.

Henry shifted his body, feeling how stiff and cold it seemed. Then he raised his hands, which were crossed over his chest, to stretch them. To his surprise, they hit a hard wooden board only several inches above his body.

At first, Henry thought he must still be asleep and dreaming. He knew of no place like this that he'd ever been before. His hands groped around to feel what kind of place it was. The more he examined it, the more he came to realize that he was in some sort of wooden box.

The air suddenly seemed heavier around him than before. Henry's mind raced through the possibilities. He could think of no other reason why he might be in a wooden box than if . . . if it were a coffin.

Through the panic creeping into his brain, Henry remembered that if he were in a coffin, he would be dressed in his best clothes, not the nightclothes of a sick man. With a sinking heart, he passed his hand over the smooth silk tie lying on his chest with his big diamond stickpin fastened through it. He remembered that he had written that request in his will — that he be buried with his diamond stickpin.

Buried alive! Henry's mind sank into horror. The doctor must have thought him dead and buried him alive. He was not dead, but dead he would surely be in a few more hours.

Henry pushed up his knees against the coffin lid. It didn't budge. He thought of the six feet of earth piled on top of him. Nothing he could do would move that weight.

A scream of despair rose in Henry's throat and echoed off the walls of the coffin. He didn't know how he could endure the slow, horrible death that awaited him.

And then, through the thoughts that tortured him, came a sound, a sound of something moving above him. It scratched against the dirt, with sharp, steady movements.

Every muscle in Henry's body tensed. What could be working through the ground of a graveyard with such persistence? Suddenly, Henry remembered horrible tales of graveyard rats. People said these rats were as big as cats. They dug down to freshly buried coffins. Then they chewed through the wood to get to the corpse inside. Henry shook with fear as the digging sound above him came closer and closer. He felt the air in the coffin become thicker and hotter. Now he had to face the choice of two terrible deaths.

Suddenly, there was a dull scratch against the top of his coffin lid. Henry imagined how big a rat must be to make that sound. He tried to push up against the lid, but it was fastened tight. He would have to lie there, like a helpless victim, until the rats had gnawed through the lid.

There was more scratching against the lid. Then, out of the darkness above him, Henry heard a voice.

"We've almost got it now," the voice said.

"All that's left is taking off the lid," a second voice added.

Henry's body froze in shock. It wasn't rats that were after his body. It was grave robbers! He heard a crowbar being wedged under the coffin lid. Then, with a creak, it started to raise up.

"You reach in for the diamond stickpin," the first voice said. "Uncle Henry paid thousands for it. It must be worth a fortune by now."

"No use letting it sit on a corpse," the second said.

Just then, the coffin lid worked loose. The two young men pulled off the lid and stared down at the corpse of their uncle. And as their greedy hands reached down to grab for his stickpin, Henry Archer rose out of his coffin and pulled them down into the grave.

He left them there, screaming with terror. Then he walked back to town, brushing off the dirt that had fallen onto his diamond stickpin.

Coming to Get You

It was one of those October nights — cold and windy — that makes you want to crawl under a blanket. But as soon as you turn off the light, you can't go to sleep. That's what happened to Beth and me. We were staying alone in her parents' cabin, which was right in the middle of a big forest preserve.

Beth's parents had driven into the city that night to go to the theater. They promised to be back as soon as possible, but that couldn't be before two o'clock. I was worried about the idea of Beth and me being all alone in that small cabin surrounded by big, shadowy trees. But Beth acted as though she wasn't scared at all.

Just before her parents left, they threw a few more logs on the fire and put up the screen. They told us to leave the fire alone and let it burn out. If we got chilly, we could just go to bed.

After they left, Beth and I sat on the big bearskin rug in front of the fireplace and played board games and talked. The fire burned fast and hot for the first two hours. Then the logs started to crumble into ashes, and the orange flames died down into glowing embers. The wind outside had grown stronger and was whistling around the house, blowing through little cracks in the walls and chilling us to the bone.

I started to shiver, although I don't think it was just from the cold. Suddenly, the idea of where we were, all alone, had started to prey on my mind. I remembered how far down the road into the forest we had traveled without seeing another house. And even during the day, the trees around the house hadn't looked beautiful and comforting. They were big pines with long, ragged limbs covered with needles. Looking out the window now, I could see their limbs flapping in the wind like ghostly arms.

"Beth, can we go to bed now?" I asked. I knew my voice was shaking, but I hoped she wouldn't notice.

"It's not that cold," she answered. "Anyway, I can make us some hot chocolate."

"Okay, but could we just take it up into the loft and drink it in bed?" I pleaded. "I like being up there at night. It feels warm and secure."

"I think you're scared," Beth said as she went to the kitchen to make the hot chocolate. "Don't worry, you'll get used to being in this place at night. I used to be really afraid when I was younger, especially after that kid from town told me those stupid stories about this place."

I sat on the floor by the glowing embers of the fireplace, turning over Beth's words in my mind. What stories was she talking about? And did I want to find out? Curiosity and fear started churning my imagination into terrible thoughts. Finally, I realized I had to ask Beth about the stories before I drove myself mad.

"What stories were you talking about?" I asked, my voice shaking again.

"Just forget it. I don't want to think about them. Here's the hot chocolate. Help me carry it up to the loft. We can crawl under the covers there. Anyway, it's always warmer right under the roof."

As Beth turned off the lights in the cabin, I walked over to the ladder that led up to the small sleeping loft. The loft was a wooden platform built across one part of the room's high ceiling, which came to a peak on top. I scrambled up the ladder first, suddenly feeling as though I had to get away from something that might be chasing me. I reached down and took the two cups of hot chocolate from Beth's hands. Then she followed me up the ladder.

We settled into the thick goose-down comforters on the loft floor. There was a small window beside us that looked out into the tall trees of the forest. Several of the trees were only feet away from us where we sat in the loft.

"Look, a full moon," I said, gazing at the silvery disk in the sky.

"Oh," Beth said with a sudden gasp. "I didn't know it was time for a full moon."

"What's wrong?" I asked, turning my worried eyes to her. "Does it . . . does it have something to do with the stories?"

"Forget I mentioned them," Beth said sharply. "Just forget it!"

I turned away, feeling angry, and stared out the window. We sat in silence for a while, both not wanting to be the first to talk.

Then, suddenly, we heard something that made both of us stare at each other with wide eyes. It was a clawing sound, a clawing sound on the outside timbers of the house.

SCRITCH. SCRITCH. SCRITCH.

For a few moments, I was too scared to say anything. I just sat there, waiting for the sound to come again. But I heard nothing — nothing but the moaning of the wind through the trees.

"Did you hear that?" I asked Beth. "What was it?"

Beth just scrunched down further under the comforter. By the moonlight, I could see her face. It looked scared.

The sound came again.

39

SCRITCH. SCRITCH. SCRITCH.

This time it was on another side of the house, by the front door.

"Beth, did your parents lock the front door?" I asked, my voice choking with fear.

"Yes," she said. "And I double-checked it."

I could tell how scared she was. Her voice sounded tight and strange as though she was feeling really sick.

"Oh, no," she said suddenly and grabbed my arm. "The kitchen window. I remember seeing that it was open a couple of inches. My dad forgot to close it after he burned the steak tonight. Oh, no, what if that thing keeps moving around the house? It could get in through the window."

I started to feel even sicker. "We've got to go down and close that window," I said, reaching over and shaking Beth. "Come on, you've got to come with me!"

I dragged Beth to her feet and crawled over to the ladder. As I started down the rungs, I heard the sound again, moving around the house in the direction of the kitchen.

SCRITCH. SCRITCH. SCRITCH.

I heard a choking sob come from Beth's throat as she stumbled down the ladder after me. We stood in our bare feet on the cold floor and froze to the spot as the sound rasped against the outside wall of the house again, this time nearer the kitchen.

SCRITCH. SCRITCH. SCRITCH.

"What if it's the werewolf?" Beth said, her voice shaking with horror. "That's what the stories are about — a werewolf. He comes out on nights with a full moon."

Fear gripped my body until I felt deathly sick. But I knew I had to get to that kitchen window before whatever was out there did. I grabbed Beth's arm and pulled her toward the kitchen. The sound was louder now, coming along the outside wall.

SCRITCH. SCRITCH. SCRITCH.

We walked into the kitchen and saw the window standing open. I forced myself to walk over to it. Just as I reached up to slam down the window, I saw a hairy arm with long, pointed claws reach through it into the room. I was too afraid to scream, but Beth shrieked with horror at the top of her lungs.

I couldn't think with that hairy arm coming at me through the window. I just slammed down the window on the arm with all my might. There was a terrible howl of pain from outside. Then the hairy arm jerked away and I heard heavy footsteps running into the night.

"No, no, no!" Beth screamed out of control as we stared at the place where we'd seen the horrible arm reaching out to get us.

I don't know where I found the feeling of calm, but I reached up and locked the window. I looked out and saw a big, shadowy figure limping off into the night, howling to the moon.

"It's gone, Beth. We're safe," I said.

"But what if it comes back?" Beth said, her voice choked with fear.

"Don't think about it," I said. Then, suddenly all I wanted was to get back up to the loft. I started to run and Beth followed me. We climbed up the rungs of the ladder as fast as we could and huddled under the blankets together.

Beth was sobbing, but I finally got her to stop by telling her that the worst was over. We were safe now.

Then we heard the sound.

SCRITCH. SCRITCH. SCRITCH.

It was the sound of claws outside the kitchen walls. Then I heard the window being forced open.

SCRITCH. SCRITCH. SCRITCH.

Now the sound was moving from the kitchen toward the living room.

"No," Beth screamed. "No!"

I clamped my hand over her mouth. Maybe, I thought, maybe it can't find us in the dark. But we had to be quiet, perfectly quiet.

SCRITCH. SCRITCH. SCRITCH.

In my mind, I saw the hairy arm coming toward us through the dark. Beth was shaking so hard I had to hold her still. Then I heard the claws at the bottom of the ladder.

SCRITCH. SCRITCH. SCRITCH.

It was climbing the rungs, one by one. Beth and I huddled together against the wall. We could hear the beast coming closer and closer. Then there was a sudden flash of light through the window. It shone like a spotlight on the top of the ladder.

And I saw the hairy arm there — coming to get us.

The lights were from Beth's father's car, and he saved us just in time. It's been a long time since this happened, and I'm almost back to normal. Except at night, during a full moon, when I hear funny sounds in the house . . .

This one is a . . . Funny Fright.

Stop That Coffin

The mortician lived in a large, gloomy house on the edge of town. Jason had passed by it on his bike many times — during the day. He always stared at the long addition built on one side of the house. His friends said that was where the mortician worked, embalming the corpses and getting them ready for the funeral home. Jason always stared at the house, but that was all.

Then, one night, Jason was walking home alone from a soccer game that had been held on a field just outside of town. Without realizing it, he found himself on the lonely street that went past the mortician's house. He was shocked when he looked up and saw that big, gloomy house. Jason stopped in his tracks and stared at the windows in the addition. There were lights shining out into the shadowy evening.

Jason couldn't explain why, but he started to walk up the sidewalk toward those lights. He was overcome by an uncontrollable curiosity to look inside those windows. Maybe the mortician was at work. Maybe he would see a . . . corpse.

Because it was twilight and not totally dark yet, Jason left the sidewalk and sneaked up to the house. He was afraid that the mortician might see him, so he went from behind one shrub to another till he drew near the wing of the house with the lights on. He noticed that the shrubs were just like the kind that grew in graveyards — with hard, sharp branches that scratched.

Finally, Jason came up to one of the lighted windows. It was just by the ground and looked down into a basement room. Jason fell to his knees and stared inside. He couldn't believe his eyes. Inside the room were row after row of coffins! Big coffins, little coffins, fancy coffins, and plain coffins. But Jason didn't see the mortician, and he didn't see any corpses.

He got back up, feeling disappointed. Then he saw the door. It was slightly ajar, and it seemed to lead to the basement where the coffins were. Without thinking first, Jason crept over to the door and pushed it open. Then he began to walk down the short flight of steps into the basement.

Right away, he noticed the strange smell — a chemical smell mixed with a sweet, rotting smell. But he just took a deep breath and kept on going. He wanted to open one of those coffins and look inside. There was a fancy one close to the door. It was made of dark brown wood. Jason walked up to it and, with shaking fingers, touched the lid.

All of a sudden, he screamed. The lid had come up and hit his hand. Then it slammed back shut with a bang. Jason jumped back from the coffin. But it suddenly reared up and stood right in front of him!

With another scream, Jason jumped away. But the coffin began to move, too. It moved like a dark ghost toward him. Jason bumped into another coffin that seemed to push him forward, toward the coffin that was coming at him. But Jason jumped aside just in time and started to run for the steps that led to the door. He felt something cold and hard bump against his back. When he whirled around, he saw the big, dark coffin trying to fall on him and crush him!

Jason ran as fast as he could up the stairs. But he heard that big coffin bumping up the steps right behind him. He twisted the door knob frantically until it opened. Finally, he ran out into the night air.

It was dark now, a totally dark night. Jason thought he had escaped from the coffin as he ran down the sidewalk away from the mortician's house. But he was wrong. He felt shiny, hard wood bump against his back again. He turned around and screamed as he saw the coffin looming over him.

Jason ran even faster, faster than he'd ever run in his whole life. But the coffin kept right behind him, like a shadow of death. Jason's lungs were hurting from running so fast. He reached into his jacket pocket and tried to find the small box he'd put there.

The coffin was coming closer and closer behind him. Jason didn't know how long he could outrun it. He tried not to think what it would do to him when it caught him! Then, finally, he found the small box he was looking for. With trembling hands, he pulled it out of his pocket. He turned around and saw the coffin right behind him.

Quickly, he pulled out the thing he needed from the box. He popped the cough drop into his mouth and . . .

IT STOPPED THAT COFFIN!

Nightmare

Before Kris fell asleep that night, she went over in her mind all her plans for the next day. She liked everything in her life to be neat and orderly, and she never did anything on the spur of the moment. Tomorrow was Saturday, and she had everything planned. In the morning she was baby-sitting, in the afternoon she had to help her parents mow the lawn. Then, in the evening, she was going to her friend Jen's house for a sleep-over. She fell asleep thinking about Jen's house, which was an old bungalow sitting along the river that flowed through their town.

The dream seemed to float into Kris's mind from out of the mysterious shadows of the night. She was standing at the bottom of a staircase, looking up. The stairs were narrow and steep and seemed to wind upward forever. She started to climb them, feeling the thick Oriental carpet covering them under her feet. She was climbing and climbing. And then, suddenly, she stood before a door. The door was small and frightened her, but she pushed it open anyway, and stepped inside the room.

The first thing she noticed were the windows, covered by dark shutters. Little shafts of moonlight drifted through them, but otherwise the room was dark. Except for one candle sitting on a stand by the bed. The candle flickered and sputtered, throwing out scary shadows across the room. Kris felt her feet move across the room, and she heard the door slam behind her.

Then there was a knock on the door and a strange woman came into the room. The woman had a face as white as bone and eyes as dark as coals. She came closer and closer to Kris with her stringy hair falling across her face. And she said, "Sweet dreams . . . sweet dreams . . . " Then she reached out her hands to Kris and . . .

Kris sat upright in bed, her eyes wide open and her breath coming in short gasps. She flicked on the light on her bedstand and stared around her room. There wasn't any old woman with black eyes and stringy hair. The room was safe and warm just like it had been when she'd gone to sleep. But the nightmare had seemed so real. She had seen the woman's hands reaching out to her!

Kris squeezed her eyes shut for a second and, again, she saw the woman's face. Opening her eyes, she looked at her clock. Four A.M. Kris knew she couldn't go back to sleep. She didn't want to

49

be in that room again. And she never wanted to see the woman's face. She huddled under her covers with her eyes open and stared at the walls of her room until dawn came and her alarm clock went off.

Kris went to her baby-sitting job as planned, and she helped her parents mow the lawn that afternoon. But all through the day she thought about the nightmare. She became more and more worried about going to Jen's house for the sleepover that night. After all, she had been thinking about Jen's house before she fell asleep. Maybe there was a secret stairway in that rambling bungalow . . . a secret stairway that led up to the room.

Without asking her parents first, Kris called up Jen just before dinner and told her that she wanted to cancel the sleepover. As soon as she had made the call, she felt better. There was no way she wanted to be near Jen's house tonight . . . just in case dreams do come true.

As Kris sat down to eat with her mother and father, she told them about her change in plans. She expected them to look happy, because they always complained that they didn't see enough of her on weekends. But their faces fell when she said she'd be home that night.

"But, Kris, we made plans ourselves," her mother said. "We knew you'd be at Jen's house, so we decided to drive to the city. We're going to the opera and then staying overnight in a hotel. We've spent too much money on tickets to change our plans. Just call up Jen and say you're coming after all."

Kris saw the woman's face from her nightmare flash across her mind. She looked at her mother and shook her head. "No, I can't do that, Mom. I just can't."

Her parents looked at each other and then at Kris.

"But you can't stay here alone," her father said. "Now just be reasonable. Call your friend Jen . . ."

The ringing of the telephone interrupted what he was going to say. Kris ran to pick it up and said hello to Emily, a new girl who'd just moved into town. She'd been trying to make friends with Kris.

"You want me to come over for a sleepover tonight?" Kris said into the phone, watching her parents' faces light up with relief. "Okay, I . . . I guess so. My parents say it's all right. Sure, they'll drop me off around seven tonight. Yeah, I'll bring my sleeping bag and pillow. Okay. Bye."

Kris hung up the telephone and sat back down at the table. Her parents seemed happy about the way things had worked out. But she really wanted to stay home in her own safe room. But at least she was going to Emily's house, not Jen's. She didn't want to be anywhere near that old bungalow by the river tonight.

Her parents dropped her off in front of Emily's house at exactly seven o'clock. Kris had never thought about where Emily might live, and she was surprised to find out that it was so close to Jen's house. In fact, it was the same kind of rambling bungalow built along the river. Emily and her father answered the door and welcomed Kris in. Emily said her mother was away, but would be back before they went to sleep.

The night passed quickly, and Kris liked Emily more and more as she got to know her better. By the time the clock struck midnight, they were still wound up and laughing. But Emily's father came down stairs and said it was time for them to go to sleep.

Emily led the way up the stairs to her bedroom on the third floor. Kris walked up the narrow, steep staircase after her, feeling the soft carpet under her feet. She tried to ignore the hints of fear that were flitting around in her brain as her feet climbed higher and higher.

Suddenly, Emily stopped on the stairs and turned around to face Kris. "I forgot something important," she said. "You go on up. I'll be right back."

Before Kris could answer, Emily hurried back down the steps. Kris didn't know what to do but continue climbing the staircase. After all, Emily seemed like a perfectly nice person, and so did her father. It was just the staircase that bothered her. . . .

Kris came around a sharp bend in the steps and suddenly found herself at the top of the staircase. As she stood facing a small door, she felt tired — more tired than she'd ever been before. Her hand reached out to turn the knob, even though her fingers were trembling. As the door swung open, she walked through it like a sleepwalker, knowing what she would see inside.

There were dark shutters over the windows. And a candle was flickering and sputtering on the bedstand. Kris walked into the room and heard the door slam behind her.

Then, as she heard a knock on the door, she slowly turned around. A woman walked into the room, a woman with a bone-white face and coal-black eyes. The woman pushed the stringy hair away from her face and smiled at Kris with yellow, crooked teeth.

"So glad you could come, dear. I'm Emily's mother."

Kris began to back away from her and fell onto the bed.

But the woman still moved toward her, smiling and mumbling under her breath, "Sweet dreams . . . sweet dreams . . . sweet, sweet dreams . . ."

The woman came closer and closer. Then she reached out her hands to Kris and . . .

The Stranger

Tara's violin lessons were always in the early evening, and she could easily walk home while there was still light in the sky. But one spring evening, her elderly teacher had fallen way behind with his students.

When Tara finally finished her lesson, she could see that the sky was turning a darker blue as the sun began to set. Tara packed up her violin in its case and said good-bye to her teacher. She knew that she should call her parents and ask them to pick her up. But she had been waiting in the teacher's house for so long. She just wanted to escape into the fresh air.

Tara hurried out the door before the teacher could tell her to call her parents. It was a warm spring evening, and Tara felt as free as the birds winging across the sky. She started off for home, humming the music she had been practicing and swinging her violin case at her side.

It happened almost without Tara noticing. The

pale light in the sky faded to a deeper and deeper blue. The green trees along the street darkened until they became black shadows. Suddenly, Tara found herself walking alone through the night. She realized that she was still a long way from home. And she still had to pass by the cemetery.

Tara's heart began to beat a little faster. She told herself that she took this walk all the time — in the light — and nothing ever happened. But she started to get nervous. The street was deserted and the street lamps ended for the stretch of road by the graveyard. She wondered what happened inside it at night.

As Tara began to walk faster, her breath started to come in short gasps that made her sound scared. She glanced to her side and saw the tombstones in the graveyard, bathed in the eerie light of a full moon. Tara turned her eyes away and stared straight ahead down the dark street. Then she decided to run.

She wasn't a good runner, and soon her legs began to feel like lead weights. Her violin seemed to be getting heavier and heavier, too. Then, suddenly, she tripped over a bump in the crumbling sidewalk and fell forward, her violin case sliding ahead of her.

Tara lay there for a few seconds, too stunned to get up. Finally, she sat up and rubbed the places on her elbows that had gotten scraped. Then, out of the dark, came a voice.

"You dropped your violin," it said.

Tara froze in fear. Where had the voice come from? Then she looked up and saw an old woman, a stranger, standing there holding her violin case.

"You should be more careful," the old woman said. Her voice was weak and quavery, and she sounded more worried about the violin than Tara.

Tara slowly got to her feet, wondering where the old woman had come from. She was staring at Tara, but Tara couldn't see her face very well in the dark.

"Didn't your parents ever tell you not to walk home in the dark?" the old woman asked, handing Tara her violin.

"Yes, they do, all the time," Tara answered. "But my lesson ran late, and I . . ."

"It's all right," the old woman said. "I'll walk along with you."

As Tara took back her violin case, she got a closer look at the woman. She looked so thin in her old-fashioned dress. And her wispy, white hair straggled out from under a veiled hat. But the moonlight was so pale that Tara really couldn't see the woman's face. And she had to watch where she was walking so she didn't fall again.

"I played the violin once," the old woman said. Then she began to tell Tara about the concerts she had given. Tara listened to the old, wavery voice. And as she listened, she noticed the strange smell coming from the woman. At first she thought it was some sort of strong perfume. Then she realized that it couldn't be perfume. It was much, much stronger.

"Could I play for you now?" the old woman asked.

Tara suddenly wanted to be home more than anything. But she couldn't stop the woman's bony, old hand from taking the violin away from her. Then Tara had to wait as the woman took the violin out of its case, plucked a few strings to tune it, and finally began to play.

The first note that came from the violin sent a shiver down Tara's back. She had never heard a note like that before, not even when her teacher played. It was eerie, like something from another world. Then the old woman started to play a strange song. It rose and fell like the wind, and suddenly Tara realized that it sounded like — like the calls of ghosts in the night.

Tara wanted to go, but she couldn't leave without her expensive violin. And the old woman just kept playing. Tara looked into the cemetery at the white tombstones, and her heart began to pound with fear. She started to reach out for her violin, so she could run away with it. But just then the woman turned her face up to the pale moonlight. And Tara saw that it wasn't a face at all, but a skull.

A scream rose from deep in Tara's throat, and she backed away from the woman in horror. Then she took off running down the street toward home. But the skeleton stopped playing her violin and ran after her. Tara ran as fast as she could. Still, she could hear the rattle of the bones running after her. She ran until she thought her lungs would burst, and finally she made it to her front door.

Tara pushed open the door, and just before she slammed it shut, she heard a note — a strange, wavering note — float through the night.

Tara rushed upstairs and went to bed, never telling her parents what happened. She was afraid to say that she had lost her violin. And she wanted to forget the horrible things she had seen that night.

The next morning, Tara woke from such a deep sleep that she thought it had all been a dream. She went downstairs, not sure what had really happened the night before. But when she opened the front door, it all came back to her.

Her violin case was lying there on the step — with a little graveyard dust on top.

Mummies

It had sounded like such a good idea — staying overnight in the museum. But now Robbie wasn't sure. He was curled up inside his sleeping bag right beside a cold, hard column that held up a big stone lion. Luke and Michael were right beside him. Mr. Arnold and the rest of the class were scattered around the big room where they were spending the night.

Mr. Arnold had been teaching them Egyptian history for four weeks, and they had all learned how to write hieroglyphics and how to make model pyramids. Mr. Arnold's old friend from college, Mr. Ellerby, was curator of the museum and had invited the class to spend the night there. For atmosphere, he had said.

"Be quiet now, boys and girls," Mr. Arnold announced. "It's a great favor that Mr. Ellerby is doing for us, letting you spend the night here. I don't want any of you to leave this room, except, of course, to visit the rest room. And now Mr. Ellerby wants to say a few words."

Michael poked Robbie in the ribs and snickered. He'd been making fun of Mr. Ellerby all day.

Mr. Ellerby cleared his throat and looked around at all the children huddled in their sleeping bags. His voice, as Robbie remembered from earlier in the day, sounded dry and cracked — like the old mummies they'd seen in the Egyptian rooms.

"I invited you boys and girls here," he began, "so that you could imagine what it was like to live centuries ago, like the ancient Egyptians. But I want to warn you. The museum is a different place at night. I often wonder what happens in those rooms at night where the remains of the past lie so quietly during the day. I wonder if the mummies move under their centuries-old wrappings . . . and rise out of their cases. I never go into the mummy rooms of the museum at night. And I don't want you to, either."

Just then, one of the youngest girls in the class let out a frightened scream and began to cry. Robbie felt a lump rise in his own throat. Suddenly, he wanted to be home sleeping in his bed — not here in this drafty, old museum with its weird statues and mummies.

Mr. Arnold rushed up to Mr. Ellerby and whispered something in his ear. Mr. Ellerby smiled nervously and then apologized to the class if he had scared them.

"I know all of you will stay out of the mummy rooms," he said. "I just wanted to make sure."

Then Mr. Arnold told everyone to go to sleep. He turned down the main lights, but left a few small lights glowing.

Robbie huddled deeper into his sleeping bag as the lights were switched off. It was almost pitch-dark in the corner where he and his friends lay. But Robbie could see the lumpy shadows of the other children sleeping on the floor of the hall. It was strange, but in the dim light, they almost looked like mummies.

Robbie woke with a start, bumping his head against the stone column he was sleeping beside. In a panic, he looked around him and saw the dim lights and huddled bodies on the floor of the museum. He'd been having a dream, a horrible dream about Mr. Ellerby taking him into the Egyptian Land of the Dead.

For long seconds, the spookily lit hall seemed no more real to Robbie than his dream had been. He couldn't understand where he was. Then, as the sleep cleared from his brain, he realized that he was in the museum. And he had a problem. He had to find a rest room.

Robbie squirmed out of his sleeping bag and

crept across the cold marble floor, searching for Mr. Arnold. Mr. Arnold had said that anyone should wake him during the night if they had to go to the rest room. Robbie peered at one sleeping body after another, but none of them was Mr. Arnold. Maybe, Robbie thought, Mr. Arnold had taken someone else to the rest room. He'd probably meet them on the way.

Robbie started down the long corridor toward the rest room. It was lined with the heads of Egyptian kings, their marble eyes peering at him in the dim light. Robbie shivered. It had become colder during the night, and the cold floor beneath his stocking feet seemed to draw all the warmth out of his body.

Robbie came to a fork in the corridor that he hadn't remembered. He peered down the narrow hallway to the left and thought he saw a red EXIT sign. He turned down the hallway, even though the lighting was dimmer. He reached out his hands and felt the smooth, cold glass of a display case. There had been cases just like this in the hallway near the mummy room.

Robbie suddenly turned around and started to run. He didn't care about the rest room anymore, he just wanted to get back to the main hall where everyone else was. But as he started back down the dim hall, he suddenly walked right into a stone wall. In a panic, he felt the wall from one side of the corridor to the other. It was a dead end. Somehow, he'd gotten mixed up in the dark.

Then he saw the red glow again, the same red glow he'd thought was an EXIT sign. Robbie ran toward it until he came to a narrow door. He walked inside a room where an ancient Egyptian lamp glowed with a flickering, red flame.

The mummy room. Robbie whirled around to run. But just then, a stone slab rolled over the narrow doorway he had come through. And standing perfectly still beside the door was a mummy out of its case.

Robbie felt fear creep through his veins like a poison. He looked around at the mummy cases lying like coffins in the room. Some of the lids were still on, with the painted faces staring at him. But some of the lids had slipped off onto the floor. It hadn't been like that this afternoon, when Mr. Ellerby had taken them on the tour. The mummy lids had all been shut tight.

Robbie looked down into the open cases and saw the mummies. Their faces were wrapped in white. Robbie screamed as one of the faces rose up to stare back at him.

Then, as though he had woken them from the sleep of the dead, more mummies rose up. Robbie watched as their stiff arms reached up to pull themselves out of the cases. He shrank back against the wall as the mummies began to move toward him.

"No," he screamed out. "Help me!"

But the mummies kept coming toward Robbie, like an army of death. They closed in on him, reaching out with their stiff, white arms.

The next morning, Mr. Arnold and Mr. Ellerby searched and searched the museum for Robbie. They looked under every statue and inside every mummy case. There was only one thing they forgot to do. They forgot to count the mummies. If they had, they would have found one more than before . . . one the size of a twelve-year-old boy.

Bloody Bones

Nobody in town ever knew whether they should believe Jess Brown's bragging or not. He would sit around the town square at twilight and tell anyone who would listen about how brave he was. He was so brave, he said, that he took walks through the cemetery at night. And while he was walking, he would call out to the dead people.

"Rise up, bloody bones," he'd say.

Then, according to Jess, the skeletons would rise up out of their graves and dance around in the moonlight.

The people in town doubted Jess's stories, but nobody was willing to follow him into the graveyard at night to find out if he was telling the truth. And many people got tired of hearing him brag, talking as though he were the bravest person in the world.

"Your big mouth is going to get you in trouble someday, Jess," people said.

Jess just laughed at them, although he could

tell by the look in their eyes that they thought he was a braggart and maybe a liar, too.

The strange thing is that Jess wasn't lying at all. He wasn't a bit afraid of graveyards, and he did take walks in them at night. And he seemed to have a strange power over the bloody bones of the dead people in the graveyard. It was that power that made him so brave.

One cold, windy night, just at the end of autumn, Jess set off for a midnight stroll in the cemetery. The moon was full that night, just the way Jess liked it, because he could see the white bones dancing in its light. He walked from his house down a shadowy path that led to the old cemetery where people from the town had been buried for the last two hundred years. There were some new bones in that graveyard, but most of them were old.

Jess walked through the wrought-iron gates of the cemetery, strolling along without hesitation. Ahead of him he saw the lines of white tombstones, looking ghostly in the moonlight.

Jess walked right into the middle of the graveyard and stopped. He listened to the wind whistling around him through the trees. And then he raised his strong voice above it.

"Rise up, bloody bones," he said. "Rise up and shake."

And all around him in the graveyard, the old, dusty bones in their graves began to stir.

"Rise up, bloody bones," Jess said again, even louder.

And the old bones sat up and then stood up and then rose out of their graves.

"Rise up and shake," Jess said in his powerful voice.

Those old bloody bones rose up and began to shake all around Jess in the moonlight. The wind blew them around and made their bony hands claw at the air and their feet dance on the soggy ground of the cemetery.

Jess stood where he was, never moving. He felt big and strong, making those old bones shake like that.

"Rise up and shake, bloody bones," Jess said again, just so he could hear the sound of his own voice.

The bony skeletons seemed to jump in the air at his command, and they shook even more. Finally, Jess had had enough, and he let the old bones crawl back into their graves to rest. He started to walk back out of the graveyard toward home, when suddenly he stumbled over an old skull and fell down.

Jess picked himself up, brushed off his clothes, and looked down at the skull. It was staring right back up at him, its old teeth grinning in the moonlight.

"Rise up, bloody bones, and shake," Jess ordered the skull.

But the skull just lay there on the ground, not moving.

"I said, shake!" Jess commanded in his loudest voice.

But the skull didn't move. It just grinned at Jess.

Jess didn't like it that the skull didn't obey him. He walked over to it and gave it a big kick with his right foot. The skull bounced down the grave-yard path and then landed with its hollow eyes looking at Jess.

"Kick me, and you'll be sorry," it said to Jess through its grinning teeth.

Jess wasn't used to being disobeyed and he'd never had a skull talk to him before. It made him so mad that he gave the skull another kick.

It bounced even harder this time and landed farther down the cemetery path. As Jess walked up to it, the skull grinned at him and said, "Kick me, and you'll be sorry."

Well, Jess kicked it again, and this time it landed right near the wrought-iron gates of the cemetery. Jess walked up to it and, again, the skull said, "Kick me, and you'll be sorry."

Jess decided right then and there that he had to show this talking skull to the people in town. He gave the skull one last kick and then set off on the path that led into the little town.

Jess went from one house to the next, pounding on the doors and telling everybody that he'd found a skull that talked. The people came to their doors, grouchy and rubbing their eyes. They all told Jess that he was just telling another one of his lies, but Jess insisted that he was telling the truth. All they had to do was follow him to the graveyard, and he'd show them the skull that talked.

Some people got dressed and came out of their houses, complaining about Jess waking them in the middle of the night with a bunch of lies.

"Listen, I guarantee you I'm not lying," Jess said. "And I promise you that, if that skull doesn't talk, you can lock me in the graveyard all night."

Most of the people just laughed at what Jess said, but one man, who didn't like Jess at all, went and got a big, strong padlock from his house. He brought it along with him as the group of towns-people followed Jess to the graveyard in the windy, cold night.

As they came near the tall, wrought-iron gates of the cemetery, Jess could see the skull lying on the path just inside the graveyard. He walked up to it while the rest of the people gathered around the gates.

Jess looked down at the skull and said in his loudest, most powerful voice, "Talk!"

But the skull just lay there on the path and grinned up at Jess.

Jess remembered how he could get the skull mad and make it talk. He gave it a hard kick. It bounced over closer to where the people were standing.

"Now, say something," Jess ordered.

But the skull just stared back up at him and grinned. The townspeople began muttering to each other in angry voices.

Jess gave the skull another hard kick. It bounced high in the air and landed not far away from the man with the padlock.

"Talk, you bloody bone!" Jess screamed. But the skull just grinned. Not a word came from between its crooked teeth.

The people from town were getting angrier and angrier. The wind was cutting through their coats, and they were tired from being awakened in the middle of the night. So they decided they'd had enough of Jess and his bragging. They slammed shut the high, wrought-iron gates of the graveyard, hooked on the padlock, and snapped it tight.

Jess heard the padlock snap and ran over to the gates. He grabbed hold of the bars and started to yell at the people to let him out. But they just grumbled angrily and headed back to their warm beds in town.

As they walked away, Jess slowly sank down to the ground. He looked over at the skull. It was grinning back at him with its crooked teeth in the moonlight.

And then it spoke. "Rise up, Jess. Rise up and shake."

Then Jess felt his body begin to rise up. And he started to shake and dance all night in the cold wind of the graveyard.

Night Woods

Carter sat near the warmth of the flaming campfire, rubbing his hands together to work out the chill. It was cold, unusually cold, for October. No one in the scout troop had brought along enough warm clothes. Carter huddled closer to the fire, wishing he were at home in bed.

"Carter," the scoutmaster's voice barked out. "We need more wood for this fire tonight. It'll be pitch-dark soon. You'd better go out and gather some now. Bring back squaw wood, dead branches, anything you can find."

Carter shivered and drew closer to the fire. Why did the scoutmaster always pick on him? Just because he was the newest member of the troop, he always had to do the jobs no one else wanted.

"Carter!" the scoutmaster shouted again. "Get going."

Carter jumped up and started to walk away from the fire.

Josh, the only friend he had in the troop, came over to him and pulled off his jacket.

"Here, put this on," he told Carter, "and thanks for getting the wood."

Carter smiled and slipped on the warm jacket. Then he headed off into the woods. He knew it was no good to look for branches anywhere near the campsite. Everyone had gathered those up when they set up camp in the late afternoon. Carter headed off down a trail that led from the campsite into a stand of thick fir trees.

The trees grew close together, their narrow trunks shooting straight up toward the sky. Carter looked for dead branches on the ground, but the fir boughs above him blotted out the little light that was left in the sky. He wandered from one side of the trail to the other, picking up an occasional stick. Then, suddenly, he turned around in all directions, trying to find the trail. He couldn't see it, and he had no idea which way he had come from.

Carter started to shiver harder than before, and he pulled Josh's coat tighter around his body. He looked up at the sky and saw that it had turned inky blue. The fir trees had lost their green color and were now black shadows against the twilight sky.

Carter knew he had only a few more minutes of twilight before the sun set completely. He threw down the few pieces of wood he had gathered and began to run through the trees. In the dim light, he thought he saw the trail he had followed away from the camp. He ran down it through the trees, his mind fighting off fear.

The trail became wider, wider than Carter remembered. The moon was brighter in the sky now, and its light lit the trail like a silver ribbon through the dark woods.

Suddenly, ahead of him, Carter saw the yellow glow of a campfire. A surge of relief shot through his body. He was going to be safe after all. Carter stopped running and let his breathing go back to normal as he walked toward the fire's yellow glow. But as he drew nearer, he saw that there was only one person around the fire, a figure whose back was turned to him. He suddenly realized it was all wrong. This wasn't his troop's campfire, and the figure before him was a complete stranger.

Carter stopped in his tracks, only a few feet behind the man. He felt scared, but the fire was so warm and inviting. Carter walked forward a few more steps.

"I'm lost," he finally blurted out.

The figure in front of him slowly turned around. Carter fixed his eyes on the man's face. It was a strange-looking face with a long jaw and a wide mouth. Then the man opened his mouth and Carter shrank back. The man's teeth were long and pointed. They were the longest teeth Carter had ever seen! And they were dripping blood!

Carter heard his own scream echo through the woods. He stumbled backward as the man worked his long teeth up and down as though he were chewing something. Then Carter ran off into the woods, away from the trail into the thick trees.

Carter heard heavy footsteps crash through the woods behind him. He ran until he couldn't breathe anymore. Then he fell onto the ground and hid beneath a fallen tree. The heavy footsteps came closer and closer. They were so close that Carter could hear the raspy breathing of the man. He shrank himself into a tight ball under the fallen tree and tried to forget the sight of those terrible, long teeth.

Finally, the heavy footsteps set off through the woods away from his hiding place. Carter stood up and started to run in the opposite direction of the man's campfire.

He ran and ran through the trees with no idea where he was going. Then, just when he thought he'd fall over with fatigue and freeze to death in the cold, dark night, he saw a small log cabin ahead of him. Yellow firelight glowed through its windows, beckoning Carter toward it.

Sobbing with relief, Carter ran up to the cabin door and pounded on it with the little strength he had left. A minute later, the door creaked open. An old woman stood there, staring out at Carter.

"Help me," Carter gasped, stumbling into the cabin.

The old woman stepped aside to let him in. She took Carter's arm and led him to a chair by the fire.

"I was lost in the woods," Carter told her, "and I saw the most horrible man. He had teeth like . . . like . . ."

The old woman leaned over Carter in the fire-light.

"Were they like this?" she said and smiled.

Carter looked up and saw her long, pointy teeth, dripping with blood.

Then, just before he started to scream, Carter heard the sound of heavy footsteps coming into the cabin. And the door slammed shut — forever.

GET Goosebumps
by R.L. Stine